GIANT
or WAITING FOR THE
THURSDAY BOAT

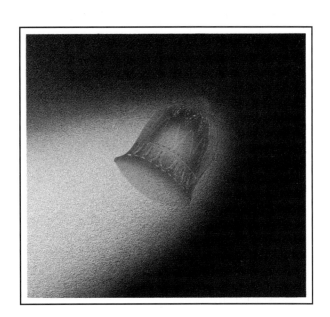

To Grandpa Thomas McKeon

© 1989 Bob Munsch (text)
© 1989 Gilles Tibo (art)
Second Printing, January 1990
Annick Press Ltd.

Annick Press gratefully acknowledges
the assistance of The Canada Council
and the Ontario Arts Council

Canadian Cataloguing in Publication Data

Munsch, Robert N., 1945–
    Giant, or, Waiting for the Thursday boat

(Munsch for kids)
ISBN 1-55037-071-5 (bound).—ISBN 1-55037-070-7 (pbk.)

I. Tibo, Gilles, 1951–   . II. Title. III. Title:
Waiting for the Thursday boat. IV. Series: Munsch,
Robert N., 1945–   . Munsch for kids.

PS8576.U58G53 1989   jC813′.54   C89-094181-5
PZ7.M86Gi 1989

Distribution for Canada and the USA:
Firefly Books Ltd.
250 Sparks Avenue
Willowdale, Ontario
M2H 2S4

Printed and bound in Canada

GIANT

or WAITING FOR THE THURSDAY BOAT

by Robert Munsch
illustrated by Gilles Tibo

Annick Press

One Sunday McKeon, the largest giant in all of Ireland, got mad for the first time in his life.

He sat under his apple tree and said, "When St. Patrick came to Ireland, he chased out all the snakes. He chased out all the elves and he chased out all the other giants. I liked the snakes. I liked the elves. I really liked the other giants. I like almost everybody, but I don't like St. Patrick."

McKeon decided to complain. He ran over the countryside moving mountains and jumping rivers until he came to St. Patrick's church. Then he pounded on the roof, yelled, screamed and smashed a few trees into match sticks. Inside the church it sounded like three earthquakes and a thunderstorm. Everybody, even St. Patrick, ran out to see what was going on.

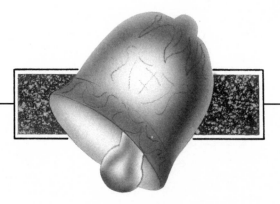

When the kids saw McKeon, they yelled "GIANT!," and climbed all over him. He let them climb for a while. Then he said to St. Patrick, "I liked the snakes, I liked the elves, I liked the giants. I just don't like you. You'll never chase me out."

St. Patrick looked at McKeon and quietly said, "I was just doing what God wanted."

"Right!" said McKeon, "Then send out your God.
I'll kick Him in the knee.
I'll knock Him on the head.
He'll never recover!"

St. Patrick laughed, "Oh no, McKeon, our God doesn't have fights with giants."

McKeon got so mad, he tore the bell out of the church steeple and threw it into the nearest ocean. When St. Patrick saw the church bell flying through the air, he said very patiently to McKeon, "You shouldn't throw church bells. Everybody knows that God likes church bells. Some day God is going to get mad."

"Good," said McKeon, "maybe if He gets mad He'll come out and fight. That would be nice:

"I'll kick Him in the knee.
I'll knock Him on the head.
He'll never recover!"

    So every Sunday McKeon threw church bells into the ocean, waiting for God to get upset.

    Finally, one Sunday, St. Patrick said, "Now you've done it. You've taken the last church bell in all of Ireland and thrown it into the ocean. God is mad, McKeon! God is coming on the Thursday boat!"

    "Great," said McKeon, "I'll meet him right on the beach. I'll pound Him till He looks like applesauce."

On Thursday McKeon sat on the beach and waited for God. The first boat to come in was a very small boat. In it was a very small girl with a lot of small fish. McKeon looked at her and said, "Did you happen to see God while you were out fishing? When He gets off His boat, I'm going to pound him till he looks like applesauce."

"I've never seen God pounded into applesauce," said the little girl. "I think I'll stay and watch," and she sat down beside McKeon.

The next boat was very fancy and had sails of silk. A rich man got off. He was so rich that he hired lots of people just to carry his money. He was so rich, he bought the ground he walked on. McKeon said, "This must be Him." He yelled, "LOOK OUT GOD! HERE COMES McKEON!"

McKeon jumped on the rich man, swung him around, and was about to throw him into the ocean when all the people yelled, "WAIT! HE'S NOT GOD!" McKeon put the man down and said he was sorry. The rich man ran off so fast, he forgot to buy the ground he was running on. Then McKeon sat down beside the little girl and waited for another boat.

The next boat was much bigger. It had lots of flags. A man came off the boat dressed in very fancy clothes. He was so important that he was carried by other people.

"Ah," yelled McKeon, "THIS MUST BE GOD!"

McKeon jumped on the man, picked him up and swung him around and around. He was about to throw him into the ocean when the people on the boat yelled, "WAIT! HE'S NOT GOD!"

McKeon said he was sorry and put him down. The man ran off so fast, he forgot to be carried. McKeon sat down beside the little girl and waited for another boat.

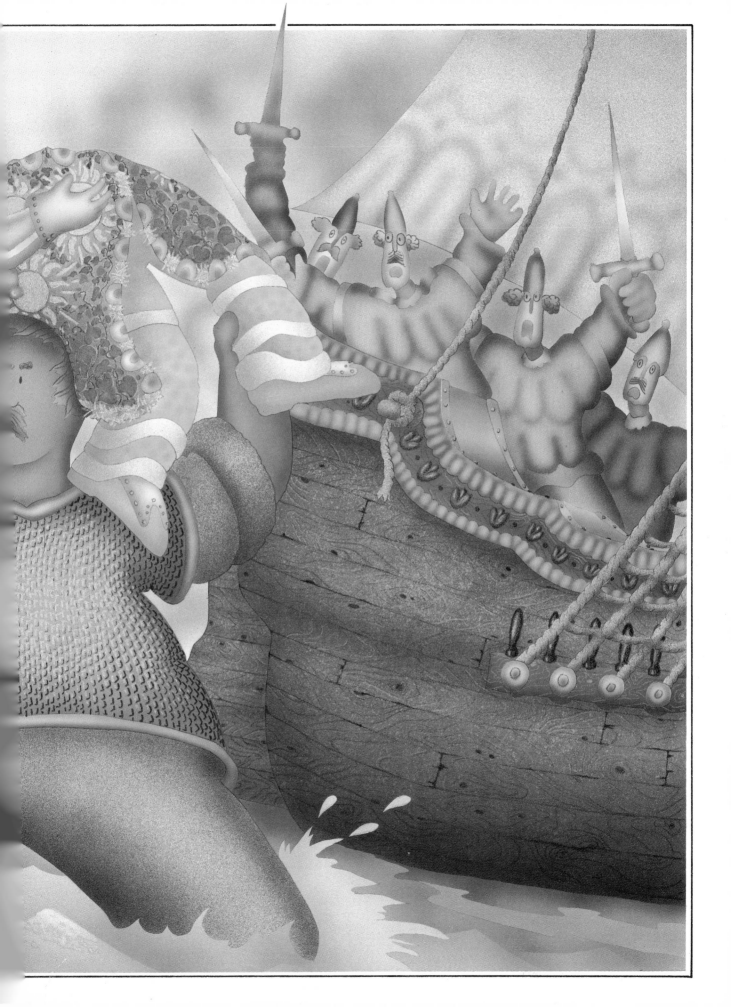

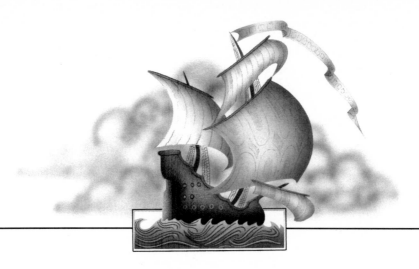

The next boat was the biggest yet. It was full of soldiers and had all sorts of flags. The largest and most important soldier got off first. He had shiny armour made of gold and silver and he rode a white horse. "Ah," said McKeon, "this is definitely God!" McKeon jumped on the soldier. Then all the other soldiers jumped on McKeon. There was a big fight. McKeon threw them all back onto the boat and told them to go fight a war someplace else.

As the boat sailed away McKeon sat down beside the little girl and said, "That wasn't God. He was too easy to beat."

"That's the last boat," said the little girl.

"I knew it," said McKeon, "God's afraid. He's not coming. He heard that I can pound mountains and move rivers and he's not coming."

"Mr. McKeon," said the little girl, "it looks like God is not going to fight. You're the world's best giant and even God would have to agree with that. Why don't you stop pounding people and go back to being friendly?"

"Good idea," said McKeon, "I don't really like being angry."

The little girl gave him three fish and they became the best of friends.

The next day, while McKeon was sitting under his apple tree, the little girl ran up and said, "Have you heard? St. Patrick has gone to heaven. He's chasing out all the snakes and elves and giants and filling the place up with church bells."

McKeon jumped up and yelled, "LOOK OUT, ST. PATRICK!"

He picked up the little girl and jumped so high his head slammed into a cloud. He jumped again and went so high he bumped into a star. He jumped again and went so high he landed in heaven. In fact, he landed right beside St. Patrick.

McKeon looked around and saw more church bells than he had ever seen before, even more church bells than in Ireland. There were no giants, no elves, no snakes, but lots of church bells. He ran off, moving mountains, jumping rivers and throwing bells over the side of heaven.

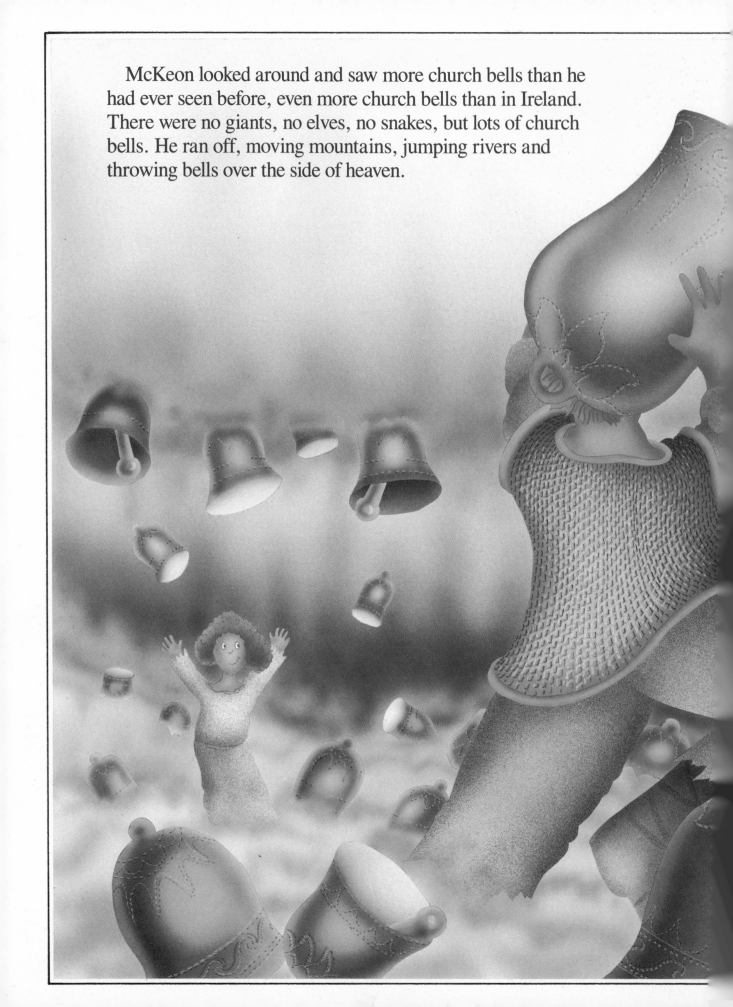

St. Patrick was very upset. He decided to complain.
He went to the biggest house in heaven and yelled,
"SEND OUT GOD!"
Nobody came out.

He went to a smaller house and yelled,
"SEND OUT GOD!"

Nobody came out.

St. Patrick tried lots of big houses and couldn't find God any place. He was so upset he sat down and cried. Just then McKeon came along and said, "Paddy, why are you sitting here crying? You're supposed to be hanging church bells."

"Ah, McKeon," said St. Patrick, "I can't find God and I want to complain about having a crazy giant like you in heaven."

"Well," said McKeon, " the smallest house in heaven has an angel out front. That's the place to go. You can complain about me and I'll complain about you."

They both went to the smallest house in heaven and, sure enough, there was an angel. They both went in and saw lots of giants, lots of snakes, lots of elves, lots of church bells...

. . .and the little girl.

She looked at them and said, "Saints are for hanging up church bells and giants are for tearing them down. That's just the way it is. Why don't you two try getting along?"

"Right," said McKeon, "I'll tear down all the church bells in heaven. Then we'll get along." He started laughing.

"Right," said St. Patrick, "I guess heaven has enough room for everyone, even giants." He started laughing.

"Oh," said the little girl, "It's so nice to have a perfect Giant and a perfect Saint."

Then she started to laugh. She laughed till the mountains shook, rivers moved and stars changed directions. For a little girl she had an enormous laugh.

McKeon is still throwing church bells out of heaven.
They become shooting stars.
Go out some night and look for one.